# HORACE MAYHEW.

SCULPTURED BY H. G. HINE.

PRYOR PUBLICATIONS
WHITSTABLE AND WALSALL

PRYOR PUBLICATIONS
WHITSTABLE AND WALSALL
*Specialist in Facsimile Reproductions*

MEMBER OF
INDEPENDENT PUBLISHERS GUILD

75 Dargate Road, Yorkletts, Whitstable,
Kent CT5 3AE, England.
Tel. & Fax: (01227) 274655
Email: alan@pryor-publications.co.uk

From the USA Toll Free Phone/Fax
1866 363 9007
© Pryor Publications 2005

International Business Awards
Shortlisted 2003

First published c 1847

ISBN 1-905253-01-X

Printed and bound by
Estudios Graficos ZURE, S.A.
48950 – Erandio (Spain)

"MODELLING DONE HERE."

# OUR MUSEUM OF MODEL MEN.

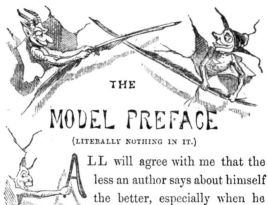

# THE
# MODEL PREFACE

(LITERALLY NOTHING IN IT.)

ALL will agree with me that the less an author says about himself the better, especially when he has nothing to say.

The quicker he says it, too, the better.

The only difficulty is where to begin. How would you possibly begin upon nothing?

Nothing easier—write a book

But if it has no beginning, it can have no end.

Precisely so—its end will be Nothing.

Thank you, Reader, for Nothing.

But it will never do for you to take me up, or my book either, in this disposition. It is too like a policeman.   Can't you be good-tempered ?

A book, to meet with its proper desert, should be gone through like a bag of filberts.  You should sit down to its contents in full anticipation of finding something good in them.  You throw away the bad ones, of course, and crack only the good ones ; these you enjoy with all the greater relish after the bad specimens, and you do not condemn the whole lot because there happen to be one or two among them not quite so sound as the rest.

Now I want you, Reader, to pick my Models in a similar spirit.  If you come to a bad one, cast it aside, and try another.  If you find nothing in that one, then select another from a richer plate, till you find something at last to your taste.   Do this kindly, in a chatty, convivial manner, as if you had made up your mind to enjoy yourself, finding fault reluctantly, and then, even, generously, and allowing the good fruit to outweigh in your judgment the bad.   Do this, I say, with perfect good humour, and, my word for it, you are qualified to sit at every literary board, gracing the richest as well as the poorest table of contents, with your presence as

THE MODEL READER.

Purchase also the book you read, and your title is complete.

Something, you see, *has* come out of nothing.

I have even something more to say.

Many of the enclosed "Models" are taken from *Punch*, that Model Publication—surely you will allow me to say that, since, in writing, it has been my Book of Models. The specimens have been all modelled from living persons. I could point to many of my friends who have unconsciously sat as the originals, whilst I was quietly plastering them on paper. If any one of them is dissatisfied with his portrait, I shall be too happy to put his name under it in the next batch.

In the meantime there is one Model which I am sure will go home to the bosom of every one who reads it, for the likeness is so self-evident that no one can fail, at the very first glance, to trace the happy identity. For this reason alone, my little book must be in the pockets of thousands, for who does not like to feel that he has that within him which brings him as near as possible to the MODEL GENTLEMAN?

This belief, once generally inculcated, would be half its accomplishment.

And now, Model Reader, if this noble end were only half attained, I ask you most emphatically if you would call that nothing?

This is certainly a Model Preface, short, modest, and all about nothing.

THE MODEL HUSBAND.

# MODEL MEN.

## THE MODEL HUSBAND

N a week day, he walks out with his wife, and is not afraid of a milliner's shop. He even has " change" when asked for it, and never alludes to it afterwards. He is not above carrying a large brown paper parcel, or a cotton umbrella, or the clogs, or even holding the baby in his lap in an omnibus. He runs on first, to knock at the door, when it is raining. He goes outside, if the cab is full. He goes to bed first in cold weather. He will get up in the middle of the night to rock the cradle, or answer the door-bell. He allows the mother-in-law to stop in the house. He takes wine with her, and lets her breakfast in her own room. He

A

eats cold meat without a murmur or pickles, and is indifferent about pies and puddings. The cheese is never too strong, or the beer too small, or the tea too weak for him. He believes in hysterics, and is melted instantly with a tear. He patches up a quarrel with a velvet gown, and drives away the sulks with a trip to Epsom, or a gig in the Park on a Sunday. He goes to church regularly, and takes his wife to the Opera once a-year. He pays for her losses at cards, and gives her all his winnings. He never flies out about his buttons, or brings home friends to supper. His clothes never smell of tobacco. He respects the curtains, and never smokes in the house. He carves, but never secretes for himself "the brown." He laces his wife's stays, even in December, and never asks for a fire in the bedroom on the most wintry nights. He respects the fiction of his wife's age, and would as soon burn his fingers as touch the bright poker. He never invades the kitchen, and would no more think of blowing up any of the servants than of ordering the dinner, or having the tray brought up after eleven. He is innocent of a latch-key.

He lets the family go out of town once every year, whilst he remains at home with one knife and fork, sits on a brown holland chair, sleeps on a curtainless bed, and has a charwoman to wait on him. He goes down on the Saturday, and comes up on the Monday, taking with him the clean linen, and bringing back the dirty clothes. He checks the washing-bills. He pays the housekeeping money without a suspicion, and shuts his eyes to the "Sundries." He is very easy and affectionate, keeping the wedding anniversary punctually; never complaining if the dinner is not ready; making the breakfast himself if no one is down; letting his wife waltz, and drink porter before company He runs all her errands, pays all her bills, and cries like a child at her death.

HE lives in chambers. He is waited upon by an old laundress, who lives he scarcely knows where. He sees her once a-week to pay her wages; but hears her every morning putting his room to rights. He rises late. He is skilful in lighting a fire—his practice generally of a morning. He understands the principle of boiling a kettle, and can cook a chop and trim a lamp. He bears all misfortunes with equanimity, and goes out without an oath to take his breakfast at a coffee-shop, if he is "out of tea." He is not astonished if he finds no loose silver in his trowsers, after they have been brushed. He has lost the keys of his drawers. His tea-caddy is, also, open from morning to night, the lock being, like his means, dreadfully hampered. He is uncertain about the number of his shirts. He has not seen a button for years. He cannot tell who drinks the grog, or what becomes of all the empty bottles. He wonders who has taken all his Waverley Novels, excepting the second volume of the *Pirate*. He is allowed only one pair of boots *per diem*. If he wants a clean pair he must clean them himself, or wait till the following morning. His washerwoman mends his linen—at least she charges for it. He takes everything good-humouredly, but is a little put out if he finds he has left his latch key in his other coat, and that he cannot get in. He is a little ruffled, also, when he discovers the laundress has not made his bed—on Christmas-day, for instance He plays only two instruments—the flute and the cornet-à-piston. He is much sought after in society, and is a great diner-out. He can tie his handkerchief in a hundred different ways, and cuts an orange into the most impossible patterns. He is a good hand at carving, and rarely sends a goose into the opposite lady's lap. He makes excellent rabbits on the wall to amuse the children, and allows them to climb up his knees, reckless of his trowsers, and hang on his neck without a groan. He shines most at a supper party. He brews a bowl of punch, and mixes a lobster salad better than any man—so he says at least. He sings a good song with a noisy chorus, and makes a speech without being "unaccustomed to public speaking." He runs through a person's Health neater than anybody else, and serves up a Toast in the most glowing style, but does not stuff a society with nothing else all the evening. He is amiable to the fair sex, and hands cups of tea and glasses of negus, without spilling them. He is in great demand as a godfather and keeps a silver mug on hand, ready for the occasion. He enjoys his comforts, but doesn't dine at home, for he has no cook. He studies his ease, but jumps up readily on a cold morning to answer the door, if the knock is repeated more than three times. He knows where the best dinners are to be had about town, and is intimate with the shops for the best meat, the best fish, the best game, the best cigars, the best everything. He walks up the stairs of his Chambers in the dark, without falling, or trying at the wrong door. He prides himself on knowing a good glass of port. He is a favourite stalking-horse of the husbands, who are never out late but they are sure to have been with him. Every "glass too much" is put down to him ; every visit to the Docks; all the half-prices at the theatre; all the dinners and suppers, no matter where, are at his persuasion. The wives consequently bear him no great affection, and generally convey their opinion by coupling his name with the prefix " *That*," very strongly italicised. His good-humour, however, conquers them, and he is welcome at every family table. He sees everything, is seen everywhere, and scarcely cares anything for anybody—excepting himself. His great object of life is enjoyment, and he succeeds to his heart's content.

Suddenly he is missed. He is not seen for weeks. He is entombed alive in his dreary Chambers with the gout, and only his laundress to tend him at distant intervals. The long days, the never-ending nights, the racking pain, the cross old woman, who makes a favour of everything and is grateful for nothing, the want of comforts, the utter homelessness of the place, strike a chill into his heart, and he would willingly give all his past enjoyments for one kind voice to cheer him, for one person whom he loved to be near him. He rises from his bed an altered man.

He finds out a young niece whom he has never seen. He buys a house and gives it to her, to allow him to live in it. She nurses him in all his sicknesses, and bears all his ill-humour. He leaves her his little property, is as kind to her as the gout will allow him to be, and is lamented at his death by one person at least.

Thus lives and dies the MODEL BACHELOR.

H E dresses in black, with a white neckcloth. He never goes to the theatre. He is not fond of cards, though he takes a hand occasionally at whist to please his old father; but then it is only for penny points. He has no talent for running in debt, or any genius for smoking. He does not flirt, or read light publications, or have noisy friends to call upon him. He pays ready money for everything, and insists upon discount. He has a small sum in a particular safe Bank, somewhere. He dances but seldom, and then only with young ladies with a very certain income. He does not care much for beauty, and has a soul above pins and rings. He never keeps the servants up, and has a horror of reading in bed. He decants the wines, and compliments his father adroitly upon his "tawny old port." He carves without spilling any of the gravy at table, and is very obliging in executing all paternal errands and commissions. There is rarely more than one Model Son in each family; but he does duty enough for half-a-dozen, as he is continually being held up as the very model of perfection to the other sons, who bear him no very violent love in consequence. His virtue has its reward in his father's will

# THE MODEL POLICEMAN.

E walks upright, as flexible as a kitchen poker, his thoughts and hands quite full—like the King of Prussia—of his "beloved Berlins." He keeps his eyes straight before him, even if there is a leg of mutton from the baker's running the opposite way. He rarely looks lower than the parlour windows, when the servants are on board wages. His heart—unlike himself—is constantly "on the beat." His taste for beauty is only equalled by his appetite for cold beef. He shows the weakness of his body by calling Daniel Harvey "Wittles."

The Model Policeman moves only in the most fashionable areas. He is rather particular in seeing if the coal cellar is fast, about supper time   He is

THE MODEL POLICEMAN

never inside a kitchen, unless "the street-door has been left open." He is affable to the footman, and smiles to the page, but suspects the butler, and calls the French maid "proud." His appearance and spirits are greatly regulated by the neighbourhood In Belgravia he wears straps, plays with a pink, and buzzes to himself some popular tune. In St. Giles's his cheeks get hollow, his buttons grow rusty, his belt is put on anyhow, and his boots are only polished with blacklead!!

The Model Policeman arrives at a row before it is quite over, and sometimes gets at a fire a minute or two before the fire-escape. He knows every pick pocket in the world, and has seen everybody who is taken up two or three times before. He has a vivid recollection of what another Policeman remembers, and if the testimony of an Inspector is impugned, he shows a great love for his cloth by swearing (as the saying is) "till all is blue." He objects to "plain clothes;" he thinks them not uniform, and "unper fessional." He never smiles when inside a theatre, nor sleeps at a sermon, nor takes an opera-glass to look at the ballet when stationed in the gallery of Her Majesty's. He rarely releases the wrong person he has taken into custody for disturbing the performances He has a virtuous horror of Punch and Judy, and insists upon the India rubber Brothers "moving on" in the midst even of the Human Pyramid. He never stops at a print-shop, nor loiters before a cook-shop, nor hangs about a pastrycook's, excepting to drive away the little boy's who choke up the door where the stale pastry is exhibited. He is not proud, but will hold a gentleman's horse at an emergency, and take sixpence for it. He rings bells the first thing in the morning, runs to fetch the doctor, helps an early coffee-stall to unpack her cups and saucers, pulls down shutters, gives "lights" to young gentlemen staggering home, directs them to the nearest "public," and does not even mind going in with them, "just to have a little drop of something to keep himself warm." In fact, the Model Policeman does anything for the smallest trifle, to make himself useful as well as ornamental. He never laughs. He is the terror of the publicans on Saturday nights, but is easily melted with "a drop on the sly."

He is courageous, also, and will take up an apple woman, or a "lone woman" with babies, without a moment's hesitation. He is not irritable, but knows his dignity. Do not speak to him much, unless you have a very good coat. Above all, do not joke with him when on duty. You are sure to know him by his collar being up. In that mood, he strikes first and listens afterwards. Do not put a finger upon him, for he construes it into an assault. Of the two forces he certainly belongs to the Physical, rather than to the Moral Force. He will help an old woman over a crossing; but is not very "nice" when roused, and thinks no more of breaking a head than an oath, if it stands in the way of his advancement. He is tremendous in a row, and cares no more for a "brush" than his oilskin hat. He hates the name of Chartist, and cannot "abide" a Frenchman in any shape, any more than a beggar, especially if he has moustaches   He has a secret contempt for the " Specials," whom he calls " amateurs." He rarely fraternises with a Beadle, excepting when there is an insurrection of boys, and it comes to open snowballing, or splashing with the fire-plug. He prohibits all sliding, puts down vaulting over posts, leapfrog, grottos, chuck-farthing, and is terribly upset with a piece of orange-peel, or the cry of " Peeler "

The rain does not terrify him, but still, to protect his clothes, he prefers standing under a spacious portico, or taking refuge in some friendly hall, where he is the centre of a group of listening flunkies who are waiting on their " missuses " waltzing above. Late at night, if there is a public-house open in the neighbourhood, you may be sure of finding him there, for England expects every Policeman to do his Duty where there is the greatest danger coupled with the most liquor.

He is kind, also, to old gentleman " who have been dining out." He learns their address, takes them to the door, sees them in, and calls the next day to inquire " if they got home safe !" A small gratuity does not offend him, especially if accompanied with the offer as to what he would like to drink?

He avoids a lobster-shop for fear of vulgar comparisons, and hates the military—" the whole biling of 'm"—for some raw reason; but he touches his hat to " the Duke." He rarely sleeps inside a cab of a cold night. He never lights a cigar till the theatres are over. He is a long time in hearing the cry of

" Stop thief!" and is particularly averse to running; his greatest pace is a hackney-coach gallop, even after a Sweep, who is following, too literally, his calling. He is meek to lost children, and takes them to the station-house in the most fatherly manner. He is polite to elderly ladies, who have lost a cat or a parrot, and gives directions to a porter in search of a particular street without losing his temper. He is fond of a silver watch, and he reaches the summit of a policeman's pride and happiness if he gets a silver guard with it.

There is nothing, however, he loves half so closely —next to himself—as his whiskers. It is only a good trimming from the Bench, or a ducking in one of the Trafalgar Square basins, that can possibly take the curl out of them. He would sooner throw up staff, station, and be numbered amongst the dead letters of the Post Office, or the rural police, than part with a single hair of them; for the Model Policeman feels that without his whiskers he should cut but a contemptible figure in the eyes of those he loves, even though he exhibited on his collar the proud label of A 1! Beyond his whiskers, his enjoyments are but few. He watches the beer as it is delivered at each door, he follows the silvery sound of " muffins!" through streets and squares, he loves to speculate upon the destina tion of the fleeting butcher's tray, and on Saturday night he threads the mazy stalls of the nearest market, his love growing at the sight of the things it is wont to feed on. His principal amusement is to peep through the key-hole of the street-door at night with his bull's eye—especially if any one is looking at him This is the great difficulty, however, for the policeman's clothes are of that deep "Invisible Blue" that persons have lived for years in London without seeing one. This is the reason, probably, when he is seen, that he throws so much light upon himself, as if the creature wished to engrave the fact of his curiosity strongly upon the recollection of the startled beholder, by means of the most powerful illumination. Without some such proof, the incredulous world would never believe in the existence of a MODEL POLICEMAN!

# THE MODEL WAITER

HE is single, of course. What time has he to make love, excepting to the cook, and she is hot-tempered and cross, as all tavern cooks are, and he has far too many spoons to look after to think of increasing his responsibilities with a family of children.

He is always "Coming! coming!" but rather, like the auctioneer, he is always "Going! going! gone!" for he no sooner jerks out "Coming!" than he bolts out of the room. Ask him for his name: It is "Bob," or "Charrrles." The waiter never has a surname. He takes his dinner how he can off the sideboard, or a chair in the passage. If he is very busy, he has no dinner at all. He approaches his plate to steal a mouthful, when fifty shouts of "waiter" call him

THIS PORTRAIT OF JOHN, MANY YEARS WAITER AT THE GRAPES TAVERN IS PRESENTED BY THE FREQUENTERS OF THE COFFEE-ROOM TO THE RESPECTED LANDLORD.

# THE MODEL WAITER.

away. Of many contending cries he attends to that of "money" first.

The Model Waiter never says *I*. He is quite editorial, and always says *We*—as, "*We're* very full at present, sir. *We* had two hundred dinners yesterday, sir, and three hundred and thirty-five suppers. *We* consume one hundred and sixty-nine rabbits regularly every night, sir." He puts on two "Sirs" to every answer, and an odd penny, if the score comes to an exact shilling—"Chop? yes, sir—sixpence; potatoes? yes, sir—tuppence; beer? exactly, sir—tuppence; and bread? yes, sir; makes tenpence, and tuppence makes thirteenpence—precisely one and a penny, sir." His favourite word is "nice." He recommends "a *nice* chop, with a *nice* glass of half-and-half;" or he says, "You ll find that a nice glass of port, sir," or it's "the nicest breast he ever saw." He can unravel the mysteries of *Bradshaw*, without turning over every one of the tables two or three times, and he knows all the play-bills of the evening by heart. He never calls a slice of Stilton "*a* cheese."

He is impartial in the distribution of the "paper," and gives the middle sheet invariably to him who has eaten the most dinners in the house. He shows no favour either with the evening papers, but awards them first to those who are drinking wine, to the spirits next, whilst to the beer he gives the Supplement of yesterday's *Times*.

His shoes are perfect fellows, with upright heels, and the strings are carefully tied; and his handkerchief so white, it would do credit to a pet parson in the heart of Belgravia. He has "everything in

the house," till you cross-examine him, when the
"everything" sinks down to "a nice chop, or a tender
steak, sir." The joint is always in "very good cut,"
and has only been up these two minutes. He is mute
for a penny, says "thank yee" for twopence, and helps
on your coat for everything above it. Politics have no
charm for him, and he never looks at a paper, excepting
when he is waiting for the last customer, and is tired
of killing flies. The only news that interest him are
the "Want Places," and the pictures. He is good-
humoured, and laughs at any joke, even those of a
Fast Man. A stranger in his vocabulary is a "party."
He talks of persons according to the boxes they sit
in, and cuts down all gentlemen to "gents." He is
not mean with his mustard, or the vinegar-cruets, and
does not hide them in a dark corner. He carries a
lofty pillar, quite a falling tower, of plates, without
dropping anything out of them, and does not spill the
gravy down an old gentleman's neck. If anything is
done to rags, or to a cinder, or under-done, or not
done at all—if the punch is as weak as water, or
there's too much sugar in it, or it's as sour as a pew-
opener, he bears it all with unruffled meekness, and
only begins wiping down the table with his napkin.
If the wine is too old, or too young, or too fruity, or
too tawny, his waiter's fine instinct tells him at once
what a gentleman will like, and he rushes out furiously
in a waiter's gallop to get it, and returns with something that elicits "Ah! that's just the thing." However, as a general rule, the port has never been less
than ten years in bottle. The cigars, too, are imported

direct from the Havannah, and cost us full 32*s.* a pound, sir. We do not clear a farthing by them, sir.

The Model Waiter very seldom has a holiday. If he does, it is to see some other waiter, or to help at the Freemason's, or to assist a friend at some grand dinner in a nobleman's family. His life vibrates between the kitchen and the parlour, and he never sits down from morning till long past midnight. He attempts to doze sometimes, but the loud chorus of "We won't go home till morning!" wakes him up, and he execrates in his heart the monster who ever composed that song; it must have been some wretch, he is sure, who owed a long score to an unfortunate waiter, who had sued him for it. He makes a faint effort to turn off the gas, but is repulsed with an unanimous call for "more kidneys." It is not wonderful, therefore, if in the morning he yawns over the knives and forks, and drops several involuntary tears whilst replenishing the mustard-pot.

After wearing out innumerable pairs of shoes, a testimonial is got up for the Model Waiter by the "gents of his room," and they present him with a full-length portrait of himself, "as a slight token of their warm appreciation of his unfailing civility, cheerful demeanour, and uniform attention during a term of forty years." This testimonial represents him in the act of drawing the cork of one of the ten years' bottles of port for a party of gentlemen who are sitting in a box in the corner of the picture, and who are portraits of Messrs. Brown, Robinson, and Smith, three of the oldest chop-eaters of the house! It is hung in a glittering frame over the mantel-piece of the room, in and out of which he has been running for the last forty years, and becomes the property of the establishment, there being a special clause let in the frame, that it is never to be removed from the room The Model Waiter, however, has been saving a little fortune of pennies during his long career of chops and steaks—his only extravagances having been the washing of his white handkerchiefs and Berlin gloves every now and then on state occasions—and he purchases, in his grey old age, the business of his landlord, takes unto himself the pretty barmaid as his wife, and dies without having once been fined for keeping open half a minute after twelve on a Saturday night, or serving a pint of beer on Sundays during the hours of divine service. His portrait still hangs over the mantel-piece as a moral public-house sign to all future waiters, that, to become landlords, they have only to keep in view the MODEL WAITER

# THE MODEL MAGISTRATE.

HE is a barrister with a subdued practice, and but little known beyond the usher of his Court. He learns, however, that the scales of Justice have two sides—one for the rich, one for the poor. The balance, as he holds it, is rarely equal. For the one there is a fine, "which is immediately paid;" for the other there is the House of Correction, with hard labour. The gentleman is invited to a seat on the bench; the pauper is kindly informed that "he had better mind what he is about." He knows the intrinsic value of every assault, and has fixed a market price for every limb. An eye costs very little more than a case of drunkenness. A broken head he puts down at a couple of sovereigns, or a donation to the poor-box. He is sorry to see young gentlemen, "who have been dining out," forget themselves so, and will only fine them five shillings this once. He is sure he has seen every applewoman before. He will have no trading on the kerbstones. He has great faith in the words of the police, and calls them by their real names. He has a just hatred of a cabman, only to be equalled by his profound aversion for an omnibus-conductor. He sees a poacher in every smock-frock.

All beggars he sentences to the Mill. He addresses a pickpocket as "Sir," and is sarcastic upon boys, calling them "young gentlemen." He delights in summoning overseers, and beadles, and enjoys a good collision with the workhouse. He regrets exceedingly to commit a nobleman. He has a private room for a lady shoplifter, and is glad to inform her that she "leaves this Court with her character quite unim pugned," though the matter has been compromised within his hearing. He has the most sublime contempt for the opinions of the press. He does not care what they say of him, though he does inveigh sometimes rather strongly against them. He does not like his law to be questioned, but of the two evils prefers a lawyer to a barrister. He jokes sometimes, and it must be confessed the joke is of the very smallest quality, but the whole Court, excepting the poor devil at whose expense the lugubrious witticism is cut, laughs tremendously.

The Model Magistrate arrives at the Police Office at ten, but does not mind keeping the Court waiting. He leaves as soon as he can, though he is not very partial to visits at his own residence. But what he likes least are remonstrances from the Home Office, for, strangely enough, a Magistrate has been dismissed before now. This may have some little influence in keeping the race of Model Magistrates rather restricted. May it soon become extinct! It is most pitiful to hear of a Magistrate committing himself as well as the prisoner!

"TAKE AWAY THE PRISONER, AND BRING IN THE DINNER."

## THE MODEL LABOURER

HE supports a large family upon the smallest wages. He works from twelve to fourteen hours a-day. He rises early to dig in what he calls his garden. He prefers his fireside to the alehouse, and has only one pipe when he gets home, and then to bed. He attends church regularly, with a clean smock-frock and face on Sundays, and waits outside, when service is over, to pull his hair to his landlord, or, in his absence, pays the same reverence to the steward. Beer and he are perfect strangers, rarely meeting, except at Christmas or harvest time; and as for spirits, he only know them, like meat, by name He does not care for skittles. He never loses a day's work by attending political meetings. Newspapers do not make him discontented, for the simple reason that he cannot read. He believes strongly in the fact of his belonging to the "Finest Peasantry.' He sends his children

THE MODEL LABOURER.

to school somehow, and gives them the best boots and education he can. He attributes all blights, bad seasons, failures, losses, accidents, to the repeal of the Corn Laws. He won't look at a hare, and imagines, in his respect for rabbits, that Jack Sheppard was a poacher; and betwixt ourselves, thinks Messrs. Cobden and Bright very little better He whitewashes his cottage once a-year. He is punctual with his rent, and somehow, by some rare secret best known by his wages, he is never ill He knows absolutely nothing beyond the affairs of his parish, and does not trouble himself greatly about them. If he has a vote, it is his land lord's, of course. He joins in the cry of "Protection," wondering what it means, and puts his X most innocently to any farmer's petition He subscribes a penny a-week to a Burial Society. He erects triumphal arches, fills up a group of happy tenants, shouts, sings, dances—any mockery or absurdity, to please his measter. He has an incurable horror of the Union, and his greatest pride is to starve sooner than to solicit parish relief. His children are taught the same creed. He prefers living with his wife to being separated from her. His only amusement is the Annual Agricultural Fat-and-Tallow Show; his greatest happiness, if his master's pig, which he has fattened, gets the prize. He struggles on, existing rather than living, infinitely worse fed than the beasts he gets up for the Exhibitions—much less cared about than the soil he cultivates, toiling, without hope, spring, summer, autumn, and winter, his wages never higher—frequently less—and perhaps after thirty years' unceasing labour, if he has been all that time with the same landlord, he gets the munificent reward of six-and-two-pence, accompanied, it is true, with a warm eulogium on his virtues by the president (a real Lord), for having brought up ten children and several pigs upon five shillings a-week. This is the MODEL LABOURER, whose end of life is honourably fulfilled if he is able, after a whole life's sowing for another, to reap a coffin for himself to be buried in!

# THE MODEL AGITATOR

HE is born with the bump of Notoriety  This bump first expands at school. He heads all the rows His special delight is in teasing the masters.  As for punishments, they only whip him on to renewed rows. He is insensible to the cane, quite callous to the birch. At home the bump grows larger.  He bullies the servants, and plays the democrat to his younger brothers.  He is always in open rebellion with "the governor," and very seditious on the question of latch keys. His love of talk bursts out on every little occasion. He will not ring the bell without an argument. He is very rich in contradictions, having always a No for everybody else's Yes. At last he revolts against parental tyranny, and is kicked out of doors. He is an injured man, and joins a debating club. The bump gets bigger. He attends a public meeting. The bump enlarges still more. He is called at the bar, and the bump has reached its culminating height. Henceforth He and Notoriety are two inseparables. He runs after it everywhere, and eventually, after numerous dodges through bye-lanes, and heaps of mud, and narrow, dirty courses, and the most questionable paths, he catches the dear object of his pursuit. He is notorious! He has good lungs, and his reputation is made. He is a hearty hater of every Government. In fact he is always hating. He knows there is very little notoriety to be gained by praising.

The only thing he flatters is the mob. Nothing is too sweet for them; every word is a lump of sugar. He flatters their faults, feeds their prejudices with the coarsest stimulants, and paints, for their amusement, the blackest things white. He is madly cheered in consequence. In time he grows into an idol. But cheers do not pay, however loud. The most prolonged applause will not buy a mutton-chop. The hat is carried round, the pennies rain into it, and the Agitator pours them into his patriotic pocket. It is suddenly discovered that he has made some tremendous sacrifice for the people. The public sympathy is

first raised, then a testimonial, then a subscription.
He is grateful, and promises the Millennium. The
trade begins to answer, and he fairly opens shop as a
Licensed Agitator. He hires several journeymen with
good lungs, and sends agents—patriotic bagmen—
round the country to sell his praises and insults, the
former for himself, and the latter for everybody else.
Every paper that speaks the truth of him is publicly
hooted at; everybody who opposes him is pelted with
the hardest words selected from the Slang Dictionary
A good grievance is started, and hunted everywhere.
People join in the cry, the Agitator leading off and
shouting the loudest. The grievance is run off its
legs; but another and another soon follows, till there
is a regular pack of them. The country is in a continual ferment, and at last rises. Riots ensue; but
the Model Agitator is the last person to suffer from
them. He excites the people to arm themselves for
the worst; but begs they will use no weapons His
talk is incendiary, his advice the very best gun
powder, and yet he hopes no explosion will take
place. He is an Arsenal wishing to pass for a Baby
linen warehouse. He is all peace, all love, and yet
his hearers grow furious as they listen to him, and
rush out to burn ricks and shoot landlords. He is
always putting his head on the block. Properly
speaking, he is beheaded once a quarter.

A Monster Meeting is his great joy, to be damped,
only, by the rain or the police. He glories in a
prosecution. He likes to be prosecuted. He asks for
it: shrieks out to the Government—" Why don't you

prosecute me?" and cries, and gets quite mad if they will not do it. The favour at length is granted. He is thrown into prison, and grows fat upon it; for from that moment he is a martyr, and paid as one, accordingly.

The Model Agitator accumulates a handsome fortune, which he bequeathes to his sons, with the following advice, which is a rich legacy of itself:—" If you wish to succeed as an Agitator, you must buy your patriotism in the cheapest market and sell it in the dearest."

THE MODEL TAILOR.

# THE MODEL TAILOR

HE is the most confiding of human beings. He is generous—charitable to a fault — for the destitute have only to go to him and ask for clothes, and they get exactly what they want. He gives them the best of everything—velvets, silks, the finest kersey meres—nothing is too good for them. He even feels a virtuous pleasure in the act, and is quite angry if the person whom he has clothed does not return to him afterwards, and be measured for a new suit. Far from repulsing you, he makes you welcome, and really feels grateful that you have not forgotten him. He presses you in the most tempting manner to have something new He has a lovely pattern for a waistcoat—a real Cashmere—it is just the thing for you. Will you allow him to send you home one ? He is miserable if you refuse, so take the waistcoat by all means, and

make the poor fellow happy.   He has, also, some
beautiful stuff for trowsers—just arrived from Paris—
it would become you admirably—will you let him
make you a pair?   Don't say No, or else his generous
heart will sink, and with it his high opinion of you.
His philanthropy, in fact, is unbounded; he does
good merely for the sake of doing good.   All men are
his brothers, with this exception, that he gives them
all they ask, even lends them money if they want it,
and never expects the smallest return.   He is the
Gentleman's Best Friend.

The Model Tailor, sometimes, it must be con
fessed, sends in his bill, though payment, generally
speaking, never enters into his thoughts.   But then
he is ashamed of the liberty, and apologises most
profusely for it.   He is fully sensible that he is doing
wrong, and blushes in his soul for the shabbiness he
is guilty of.   It is only that he is terribly distressed
for money, or else he would not think of "troubling"
you.   He is greatly subject to that heaviest of all
social calamities—a "little bill."   He asks you, as
the greatest favour, to let him have a "trifle upon
account," and leaves you happier than poets can
express, if you promise to let him have something
in a day or two.   Should it be inconvenient, however,
he never presses the point, and will look in some
other time.   Should you express astonishment at his
demand—you cannot have had his bill more than
two years—he excuses himself in the most penitential
manner, and begs your pardon for having mentioned
the subject.   The next day he calls to inquire if you

want anything in his way; the generous creature forgives as quickly as he forgets. His anger is only roused when you leave him to go to another tailor. He is very jealous of any one else doing a kind action, and would like to enjoy the monopoly of all the Schneider virtues. In his anger he has been known to send a lawyer's letter; but if you go to him and quietly tell him what you think of his conduct, and order a new wrap-rascal, he will settle the matter himself, and assure you that the thing is purely a mistake, and that no one can possibly be more sorry for it than he is.

The Model Tailor takes a pride in seeing his clothes on the back of a perfect gentleman. He knows no higher gratification than when he is " cutting out" a nobleman. His greatest enjoyment is going to the Opera, and recognising, from a distance, the Earls, and Marquises, and the dashing young Barts. and Knts., all walking about in the "charming" coats he has made for them. He throws his entire soul into his business, and places it high amongst the Fine Arts, Sculpture excepted, which in naked truth he thinks very meanly of, as he cannot imagine how persons can see any beauty in Apollo and Venus, dressed as they are, or how a toga can be considered a suit of clothes any more than a table-cloth.

The Model Tailor has exquisite taste, and unlimited faith. He praises the figure of every one of his customers, and never doubts any one till after four years' credit. He strives his utmost to conceal the eccentricities of a pair of parenthetical legs, and spares no cloth for fattening every miserable lean calf that comes under his paternal shears. He disowns fox's heads and four-in-hands, and such vagaries upon saucer buttons, and does not encourage the style of dress invented by the "stable mind." He warrants to fit anything, and boasts, though not much given to joking, of having made a dress-coat for a corkscrew. He does not recommend things to wash, that are sure to leave their complexion behind them in the first wash-tub; nor make a practice of registering his straps, his belts, button-holes, and every little article of costume. He estimates men, not by their measures but his own, and in his tailor's eyes he is the best man who turns out the best after he has been well dressed by him once or twice. He despairs of Lord Brougham ever being a great man, but has great hopes of Prince Albert.

The Model Tailor rarely makes a fortune, unless he has been very unfortunate through life. An insolvency just puts him straight; a first bankruptcy leaves him only a handsome surplus, but a second one enables him to retire. The sad truth is, that the simple child of Eve knows he owes all his business to the fact of her biting the apple, and he has not the heart to distress any son of Adam for the clothes he wears. Perhaps he feels that it would be like pocketing the wages of sin. His assignees, therefore, are obliged to collect his debts for him, and accordingly, the oftener he fails, the richer he becomes. He buys, in his old age, a large estate with a small title upon it, somewhere in Germany, and leaves his "goose" to

be cooked by somebody else, universally regretted by
all those customers who have known him since the
date of his last fiat.   He lives a happy Victim, and
dies a contented Baron.  Of all tradesmen there is not
one so estimable, so incredulous, so generous, so beloved, when you meet with one, as the MODEL TAILOR

# THE MODEL M.P

HE lodges in Parliament Street, but has his letters addressed to the Garrick, or Reform Club. He enters the House invariably before prayers, and only leaves it with the Speaker. He never misses a Wednesday. He even attends on a Chisholm-Anstey night, or when the Danish claims are brought forward  He

is a very great man at the hustings, making the most
lavish threats to amend the Constitution and stop the
supplies; but somehow, when he gets into the House
he sinks into one of those Hon. Members whose voice
is always "inaudible in the gallery." He rises occasionally, but sits down directly if any other Mem
ber rises with him. He is not very ambitious, seldom
going beyond a "laugh." His favourite flight is to
count out the House on a Derby day. He has not a
large conscience. He votes unremittingly with
Ministers, and has his reward in a gracious bow from
Lord John, and occasionally an invitation to dinner,
when he is quite proud to see his name in print, and
dispatches innumerable copies of the paper to his
constituents.

He has a profound veneration for the British Lion,
and loves to display his classical knowledge by applaud-
ing every little bit of Latin and Greek. He is deeply
skilled in the Parliamentary gamut, which he can run
up and down with the zoological flexibility of a Von
Joel, from a crow in C major to a donkey in D alt.
He is an easy victim for a Committee, and takes a
pride in attending the deputations of the Commons
before the Lords. He is a stern upholder of the
etiquette of the House, and is fond of summoning
innocent printers before the bar, or of incarcerating
Irish Members in coal-holes, for contempt. He
executes the little errands of his party, and on an
emergency acts as whipper-in. He sups regularly at
Bellamy's, where his profound knowledge of chops
and steaks is highly respected, and his calls for "lemon

peel" instantly attended to. The clerks and door keepers look up at him as a clock, and put on their great-coats and comforters immediately they see him come out.

In private life, the model M.P. attends public meetings, and seconds all sorts of charitable resolutions for the Blacks, and philanthrophic expeditions up the Niger. He has been known even to take the chair at a benevolent dinner, when the Duke of Cambridge has been absent by indisposition. He subscribes liberally to hospitals, to all charities, mock and real, to every new testimonial, and is too happy to forward any absurd plan with the full strength of his two initials. He reads every newspaper, and dies in the possession of his seat, very obscure, but universally regretted by the party which has had his vote for the last fifty years.

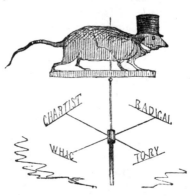

## THE MODEL DEBTOR

HE never thinks it dear so long as he gets a thing on credit. No dinner is too good for him; the dearest wines, the earliest peas, the most juvenile strawberries, the strongest liquors, the most exotic luxuries —everything that is expensive and delicious, so that he is not called upon to give ready money for it. The world pays, and he enjoys himself. His cab is found him free of expense, and by some charm he has a two hundred guinea horse sent home to him without paying a single penny for it. The rent of his house is several quarters due; the furniture is of the very best, but not a stick or a stitch of it has been settled for, and the very sheets he sleeps in might be taken from under him by his washerwoman, for terrible arrears of debt. These thoughts, however, do not trouble his happiness. He trusts, for everything, to his appearance. He knows well enough that a man with a shabby exterior never gets credit for anything in this world. He has a good coat, and on the back of it orders as many clothes as he likes. He has only to ask for hats, boots, walking sticks, pistols, dressing-cases, and they are all left at his "residence," exactly as if he had paid for every one of them. No questions are asked—not a soul is in a hurry; for "any one can see he is a perfect gen tleman." He flourishes a cheque-book, though his drafts would not be liquidated at any other bank but Aldgate Pump. The day of reckoning, however, sooner or later, comes. Then it is that the wonderful impudence, the real genius, of the Model Debtor, bursts out in all its greatness. It is not convenient for him to pay just at present. It would be ruination to sell out when the funds are so low. He wonders at Mr. Smith's impatience (Smith is his butcher)—the bill can barely have been owing two years—but he will call and settle next week. Some he threatens to expose; the impertinence of others he will certainly report to all his friends; and he silences the noisiest with a piece of stamped paper, on which his name is inscribed, as the representative of hundreds of pounds. But the bubble gets larger and larger, till it bursts. Then the Model Debtor tumbles from his high estate—if ever he had any—and from an "eligible mansion" he falls to a "desirable lodging," at a few shillings per week. He likes the Surrey side of the Thames best.

His life is now a constant game of hide-and-seek. He is never "at home," especially to top-boots and

Jerusalem noses, that bring letters and wait for an-
swers in the passage. He grows nervous. Every knock
at the door throws him back, and he rings the bell
violently two or three times, whispers to the servant
through the door, turns the key, and crouches down
with his ear at the key-hole. He looks out of the
window before he ventures in the street. He only
walks when he cannot afford to pay for a cab. Om
nibuses are dangerous: it is not so easy to avoid a
creditor inside. He selects the dreariest thorough
fares, and never penetrates into a *cul-de-sac*, or approaches within a mile of Chancery Lane. His
impudence, however, does not desert him. He never
recollects any bill whatever, and if stopt and ques
tioned about his name, he threatens in the grandest
manner to call the police. When pressed for money,
he is sure the account was paid long ago, and that he
has got the receipt somewhere at home. He is most
fruitful in excuses, and lavish in promises. He gene
rally expects a "good round sum in a day or two."
He can never get his accounts in, and was disap
pointed only last week of a large balance he had relied
upon for paying your little "trifle." As he falls lower
in the world, he gets meeker. He would pay if he
could. All he asks for is time. Business is very bad
—never was worse. He only wants to look round
him. He hopes you won't be hard upon him; but if
prosecuted, if goaded to death in this way, sooner than
lead the life he does, he will go into the *Gazette*, and
then his creditors must not blame *him* if they don't
get a farthing. He means well, if they will only leave

him alone. He will be happy to give you a bill. He has a wife and seven children. In fact, he is a most affectionate parent, and the sacrifices he has made for his family no one can tell but himself—which he does upon every possible opportunity. He grows tired of answering letters, and as for giving the name of his solicitor, he hates the law too much to do it. He meets a bill and a bailiff with equal horror ; but does not care much for either, if he can only be sure of a " good long run." He is very sensitive about the left shoulder, going off, like a hair-trigger, at the slightest touch. His great day is Sunday. He is then everywhere—in the Park especially—and any one to see him would imagine " he could look the whole world in the face, and defy any one to say he owed him a shilling." He is brave, too, during Vacation. He is very intimate with the law, and has a profound respect for the Statute of Limitations ; but thinks England not worth living in since the County Courts Act. He carries his anti pathy, indeed, so far as to run over some fine morning to Boulogne and never coming back again, leaving all his property, though, behind him in a carpet-bag replete with bricks. There his first care is to cultivate a moustache, and to procure new clothes, new dinners, fresh victims. He is always expecting a remittance by the next post. His bankers, however, are very remiss, and he is lodged at last by his land-lord in the *Hotel d'Angleterre*—in plain English, the prison. He only asks for time, and at last he gets more of it than he likes, for he is locked up for two or three years in jail, unless he is very lucky and is liberated by a Revolution. He disappears no one knows where. His friends wonder what has become of him, till there is a vague report that he has been seen as an *attaché* to one of the gaming-houses about Leicester Square, or, if he is tolerably well off, that he has been recognised on the road to Epsom, driving a cab, with a large number (say 2584) painted upon it

The Model Debtor is honest at last, for he has arrived at that stage of life at which no man will put any trust in him. He pays his way—turnpikes inclu ded—and does not overcharge more than what is perfectly Hansom. He pays ready money for every thing, even down to the waterman on the cabstand, and gives himself out as "a gentleman who has seen better days." His great boast, however, is that all through the ups and downs of his racketty career, he never left unpaid a single debt of honour. Doubt-lessly, this is a great source of consolation to the numerous tradesmen to whom he never paid a penny!

HE borrows money, of course, and pleases himself about returning it. Your house is his house—your property just as much his property. He invades your library at all hours, and smuggles what books he likes, and lends them to whom he chooses. He rides your horses, and buys Havannah cigars, and Eau-de-Cologne, and all sorts of bargains for you, no matter whether you want them or not. He has a patent for giving advice, and speaking his mind very freely at all times. He must be consulted in any step you undertake, from the purchase of a poodle to the choice of a wife. He wears your collars, your gloves, and does not mind putting on your great coat, or even, at a stretch, wearing your polished leather boots, and walking off with them. He will stop with you a month, if you ask him for a week, and will bring one or two especial friends —" capital fellows" he calls them—if you ask him to dinner In return, he is obliging, obsequious, has a wonderful capacity for drinking and smoking; tells a good story, and sings a good song; wins your money at *écarté* with the best grace in the world; will get you to accept a bill, and almost persuade you he is doing you a favour; and if you should be penniless to-mor row, he will meet you in the street, and, as a Model Friend, cut you

## THE MODEL FAST MAN

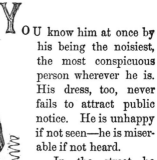

**Y**OU know him at once by his being the noisiest, the most conspicuous person wherever he is. His dress, too, never fails to attract public notice. He is unhappy if not seen—he is miserable if not heard.

In the street he flourishes a little stick, which, for want of something better to do, he rattles against the railings. He stares ladies in the face, and takes his hat off to carriages, and delights in kissing his hand to some old dowager who is looking out of a drawing-room window. A sedan-chair is his great amusement. He stops the porters, and asks them what they will take him to Buckingham Palace and back again for? He directs a hackney-coach to drive as fast as possible to the British Museum, and to ask Sir Henry Ellis to be kind enough to put it under a

THE
MODEL FAST MAN

glass-case among the Fossils. He takes a card that is offered to him by a street conjuror, and gives him in return one of his own, with an intimation that he "shall be happy to see him at any time between two and four." He walks behind fat old ladies, and is very loud in the praises " of the jolly mad bull there is in the next street." He rings area-bells and inquires " if they could oblige him with the loan of a cucumber-slicer for five minutes." He removes any pewter-pot he finds, and knocks at the door to ask " if it belongs to them : it was hanging outside the railings, and might be stolen by some unprincipled person." News-venders are his especial favourites. He calls them from the other side of the way to ask " if they have got the *Independent Doorknocker* of 1356 ; if not, he should like to see the third edition of the *Times* to-morrow." He makes cruel faces to little babies as they hang over their nurses' shoulders, and is flattered if he makes them cry. If he meets with twins, he is happy indeed. He shouts into sausage shops as he passes by—" D 'ye want any cats, dogs, or kittens, to-day ?" He hails an omnibus, and whilst it is stopping, turns down the next street ; and he looks at a cabman till he drives up to him, when he wonders what the " cabbie " wants : he was only admiring his handsome whiskers. If he finds a looking-glass he adjusts his toilet in it, and takes off his hat, and bows to himself, exclaiming, " On my word, you are looking remarkably well ; I never saw you look better." He looks at the milliners through the shop-windows, and darts at them his most piercing smiles. He stares at the watch·

makers at their work, with intense curiosity, and talks to them with his fingers, till they get up and leave their stools with great indignation. If he meets the Lord Mayor's carriage with three footmen on the foot-board, he is sure to call out "Whip behind!" and he laughs his loudest if the coachmen should uncon·sciously lay his whip across their calves. He is very rich in noises. His "Va-ri-e-ty" is unequalled at two o'clock in the morning; and his collection of "Ri-too-loorals," and "Rum-ti-oddities," and select choruses, is not to be surpassed by the oldest *habitué* of the Coal-hole. He whistles, too, through his fingers; and can bark, crow, and bray quite naturally, especially inside Exeter Hall, or any place where he shouldn't do it. One of his proudest achievements is to enter an omnibus crowded with females, and to display on his knees a large jar, marked "Leeches." He delights, too, in sprinkling cayenne-pepper and snuff on the floor of a dancing-party after supper, or in going behind the cornet-à-piston, and making him laugh during a long solo, when the struggling laughter oozing out in short gasps through the valves, nearly sends him into fits. He glories in sending in six "brandies warm" to the chairman and different gentle-men on the platform of a Temperance Meeting. He makes a practice of ringing the bells of all doctors as he walks home at night.

In the theatre, he slams the box-door, and shouts "Box-keeper!" with the most stentorian lungs. He is vociferous in his applause, and sparkles up at the prospect of a row. He likes to sneeze during the pathetic parts, and shouts " Brayvo, Wright!" when the old father is blessing his long-lost child. He revels in a burlesque with plenty of Amazons in it. He cries out " *Encore!* " at everything, but Hicks especially.

In respectable society he is awkward, and generally very quiet. He does not dance, not knowing what to say to his partner. He hangs about the door and staircase, and consoles himself with the cakes and wine; he leaves early, for " he is dying for a pipe and a drop of beer."

In his appearance he selects the gayest fast colours, and the more the merrier. His shirt is curiously illuminated with pink ballet-girls. He has the winner of the Derby in his pocket-handkerchief. His boots are very delicate, only keeping body and sole together with the aid of large mother-of-pearl buttons. He revels in a white hat. His trowsers are of the chess-board pattern. His shirt-pin is an Enormous Goose berry, that would make the fortune of a penny-a-liner His coat has a Newmarket expression, of the very deepest green. He is above gloves, but encourages a glass, suspended by some magic process in his left eye.

His accomplishments are various. He carries in his waistcoat pocket the stump of a clay pipe, the bowl of which is quite black. He can walk along the parapet of Waterloo Bridge. He can sleep in the station-house upon an emergency. He can slide, skate, and box a little, and play the French horn. He can win a game of billiards, and give you twenty. He is " up to a dodge or two " at cards. He can imitate all the

actors, and a brick falling down the chimney. He can
fry a pancake in his hat, and light a cigar at a lamp-
post. He can manage a pair of sculls, and tool a tandem
through Smithfield Market. He can talk slang with a
novelist, and "chaff an 'University Man' off his legs."
He can also "do a bill," and many other things, as
well as persons, that ought not to be done. He is pro-
ficient in all the gentish graces of life, and knows "a
small wrinkle or two" of everything. High life, low
life, gambling life, sporting life, fashionable life, every
kind of life he is intimately acquainted with, particularly fast life. This consists in his beginning the day
six hours after everybody else, and finishing it six
hours later. It implies the knowledge, on his part,
of the Polka, with certain embellishments, and a con
stant attendance at Casinos, and other places where
that knowledge can be displayed. It involves, also, a
course of theatres, sporting-houses, masquerades, sing
ing-taverns, cigar-shops, cider-cellars, and early coffee
houses. To all of these the Model Fast Man is an
accomplished guide. He condemns everything as
*slow* that does not keep pace with the rapidity with
which he runs, or rather gallops, through life; and
he annihilates everybody as slow who presumes to
live like a rational creature. All books are slow—
Shakspere is slow—all domestic, all quiet enjoyments
are slow. The country is very slow, and so are sisters.
He even calls the railways slow. His great impulse
is, "Fast bind, fast find," and he sighs that society is
not bound by the same fast law. He is without shame,
as he is without gentlemanly feeling. He is familiar

with servants, is very facetious with conductors, calls
policemen by their letters, jokes with waiters, and does
not care how he insults an inferior. Impudence, to
him, is fun—brutality, the excess of refinement—
giving pain his most exquisite enjoyment. His highest
notion of humour is saying to everything, " I believe
you, my bo-o-o-o-y." In the morning—that is, the
afternoon—he is feverish ; in the evening—that is to
say, four o'clock in the morning—he is what he calls
" fresh." His first call is for soda-water, his last
for brandy. Such is the great beginning, and such
the grand end, of the existence of the MODEL FAST
MAN.

## MODEL CLERKS.

THE Lawyer's Clerk enters the office at
nine, and leaves at eight. His
only holiday is when he is sent
into the country to serve a writ.
He has a "fine bold hand," and
can "fair copy" two
brief sheets an hour
He does not throw up
his salary because he is
too proud to engross
skins of parchment; on
the contrary, he has a
pair of false sleeves (like umbrella-cases) for the pur-
pose. He knows exactly the legal price of everything, from a savage assault to a breach of promise
of marriage. He is not fond of taxing, and is ready
to cry if not allowed his "Letters and Messengers,"
every Term. His great delight in an action is to
"get costs." He then shows the admirable
system of "the office," by proving in how short a
time a long bill can be made out, sent in, execution
served, with the sheriff's sale, if not paid within a
fortnight. He has no patience with people who come
to beg for time—he is very sorry, he has but one duty
to perform. That duty is invariably an appointment

with the obsequious John Doe, made by Her Gracious
Majesty at the Court of Exchequer, or some other
place of amusement. He does not read novels during
office-hours, nor roast chesnuts, nor apples, nor act
plays, nor toss for beer, nor learn "The Wolf," or any
song, comic or dreary, when "the Governor" is out.
His soul is in his master's pocket, and he always
appeals, or has a rejoinder ready, or a new bill on the
file, if the client can only afford it. His cry, like
Demosthenes', is always "Action, action, action," and
in his opinion the best reward a good action can have
is a Chancery suit. He is cautious as he is zealous—
keeps a copy of every letter, almost dislikes saying, "How
d'ye do" without a witness, has a horror of giving
promises on paper, and always tries to inflate 6s. 8d. into
the dimensions of 13s. 4d. He would blush to take any
of the office paper home with him. He understands perfectly when a client has called to complain of delay;
in which case, " Mr. Hookham has always just stepped
out—he believes it is to move in your very suit." He
takes but half-an-hour for his dinner, and only allows
himself ten minutes for his tea. When he serves you
with a writ, he hopes "you will not be offended—
it is his most painful duty." The same with a distress; he throws a cloak of politeness over every step
that gradually leads a man from a lawyer's office to
the Queen's Bench. By half-starving, the strongest
self-denial, little agencies from friends he has recom-
mended to the office, and the Christmas Boxes of a
long range of years, he saves a hundred pounds, and,
working upon half salary in lieu of a premium, gets

articled to his master. However, the County Courts have beggared a fine profession, and Lord Brougham has so cut down the profits of the Law to barely a herring a-day, that he is obliged to come back and occupy the same stool he has grown grey upon during his clerkhood. He buries all ambition in his "pad," takes to copying after office hours, in order to gain a few pounds, when his fingers will no longer be able to hold a pen, and ultimately resigns his desk to some young man, who, like himself, with a strong constitution, and probably a generous heart, sells himself to lose both, for the matter of eighteen shillings (and "a rise") as a Lawyer's Clerk

The RAILWAY CLERK dresses smartly. He is a friend of a Director, or the cousin of a large Shareholder. Business with him is quite a secondary consideration. He opens his little trap-door five minutes before the train, and closes it the minute the clock has struck He will take your money if you want a ticket, but mind, he is not answerable for any mistake. He has no time to count change, or answer questions about trains, or attend to stupid people who come inquiring about the persons who are killed by yesterday's accident. It is not his business. He cannot attend to every one at once, and he runs his diamond fingers through his rich, Macassared hair. It's really no fault of his if you lose the train—you ought to have come sooner; and then he whips off, with a very pretty penknife, a sharp corner that pains the symmetry of one of his filbert nails. What should he know about dogs?— you had better inquire at the luggage train. You can write to the newspapers by all means, if you like: the newspapers don't pay him. The parcels are not in his department—the porters perhaps can tell. He is very sorry he has no change for a five pound note—he has no doubt you can get it round the corner. He yawns all the morning—his eyes are only half open at eight o'clock, and his white waistcoat betrays his dreadful impatience to get to the Opera, as the time draws slowly towards the mail train. What he does between the dreary intervals, as we cannot peep over the walls of mahogany into the small circle of his duties, we cannot tell. On a Sunday, however, his usual amiability deserts him. His cambric shirt is beautifully smooth, but his temper is sadly ruffled. The excursions upset him. The number of absurd questions annoy him. He wonders how people can be so foolish, and at last makes a resolution not to answer any more inquiries; and the Railway Clerk knows his own dignity too well not to keep it. He becomes as silent as a Government Surveyor's Report over a "Dreadful Collision." He only stares; but occasionally troubles himself to the utmost of his abilities to give a nod that may express "Yes" or "No," just as the person pleases. Beyond this, the Railway Clerk is as obliging as most Clerks, and he has this advantage, that he is very good-looking, and after coming out of an omnibus on a wet day, is quite pleasant to look at. In the heat of summer he looks cool—in the depths of winter he always appears warm and comfortable. He is really a pattern of politeness to ladies, and smiles most condescendingly to pretty girls, displaying his gallantry and white teeth in a thousand little ways. He was evidently intended by Nature as an ornament to a tea-party, or born to grace a pic-nic. The only pity is, that his friends ever made him a Railway Clerk

The GOVERNMENT CLERK is the most refined speci men. He has grown so mild by practice, that he never loses his temper. He knows his station better than to argue, or dispute, or contradict, or differ in opinion with any one. He has a sovereign remedy that protects him from all complaints, mild or virulent, and that is, deafness. Do what he will, he cannot hear. It is a great impediment that has often been tried, but never been cured. You must speak two or three times, and very loudly, too, before you can make him hear a single word. He has then a very indistinct notion of what you want, and must read the account of last night's farce deliberately through, and look at himself in the glass, before he can arrive to a perfect comprehension that you are in want of anything. "Oh! yes; he recollects, you wish to pay the legacy duty on the will of Mrs. Trinkumkolee, who died in the State of Nincom poopoo, in the year—he is very sorry to have kept you waiting." It is in fact in the art of putting a person off that the Government Clerk is especially clever. He does this so politely, that though offended you are yet afraid to give explosion to your anger. "He will be with you in one instant;" and he retires with a new coat into the next room to give audience

to one of his tailors. "He shall be happy to attend
upon you directly;" and he finishes to his fellow-
clerks a most curious incident that occurred to him
last night at the Polish Ball. "Will you be kind
enough to take a chair?" whilst he perfects a Sweep
for the next St. Leger. You cannot possibly be rude
with one who is so polite. At three o'clock he locks
his desk, and commences his toilet. After that hour
every one is most blandly requested to take the trouble
to call again the following day. At four o'clock, as
soon as the quarter before it strikes, he is to be seen
on the water, or in Hyde Park, or on the top of an
omnibus, so neatly attired, you never would suspect
he had been doing a hard day's business. In fact,
who can tell the papers he has diligently read, or
the tender notes he has beautifully written; or the
happy bits of literature he has knocked off for *Punch*,
or *Blackwood's Magazine;* or the heaps of "Don't
love" and "Do love," he has swept together for
gorgeous illuminated songs, if Balfe only likes to
have them; or the quires of paper he has richly car
tooned; or the endless quills he has cut into tooth-
picks, or the countless variety of things, all requiring
time, and some degree of ability, that a Government
Clerk is expected to do when he gives his presence to
his ungrateful country, from the very early hour of
ten in the morning to as late an hour as four in the
afternoon. Sometimes, also, he is a dramatic author,
that is to say, he translates French pieces, and it cannot
be pleasant to be interrupted in the middle of a most
impassioned scene, between a countess and a senti-

mental barber's boy, merely to give a stupid date, or to hand over the office copy of some dreary document. Hasn't he to keep himself clean too, all the while? for, call when you will, you always find the poor fellow busily employed in washing his hands, or combing his hair, or dusting his boots, or mending his nails. Before we laugh, we should really pause to consider whether there is any one who could do as many things so well in the same short space of time, as the Government Clerk.*

THE BANKER'S CLERK is born to a high stool. He is taught vulgar fractions, patience, and morals, in a suburban school. At fourteen he shoulders the office-quill. He copies letters from morning till night, but has no salary. He is to be "remembered at Christmas." He is out in all weathers. At twenty he is impervious to rain, snow, and sunshine. At last he gets £40 per annum. Out of that revenue he pays £5 a-year to the "Guarantee Fund." He walks five miles to business, and five miles home. He never stirs out without his umbrella. He never exceeds twenty minutes for his dinner. He drinks water; "beer gets into his head." He has three holidays a-year—Christmas

---

* CAUTION.—The above specimen refers only to the highest grade of Government Clerks—the fine gentlemen who get stupendous salaries for doing nothing, and make a favour of doing that. The poor subordinates do work, and get almost nothing for it. Promotion is hopeless without patronage—the best talent of little avail, unless you have some one with a title to make it evident for you. If you wish to bury your son alive, get him a situation in a Government Office.

Day and Good Friday being two of them—and then
walks to the office and back again to pass away
the time. He runs about all day with a big chain
round his waist, and a gouty bill-book in his breast-
pocket. He marries, and asks for an increase of
salary. He is told "the house can do without him."
He reviews every day a long army of ledgers, and has
to "write up" the customer's books before he leaves.
He reaches home at nine o'clock, and falls asleep over
the yesterday's paper, borrowed from the public-house
He reaches £80 a-year. He fancies his fortune is
made; but small boots and shoes, and large school
bills, stop him on the high road to independence,
and bring him nearer to Levi than Rothschild. He
tries to get "evening employment," but his eyes fail
him. He grows old, and learns that "the firm never
pensions." One morning his stool is unoccupied, and a
subscription is made amongst his old companions to pay
the expenses of his funeral. So much for clerkship!

"AM I NOT A MAN AND A BROTHER?"

# THE MODEL GENTLEMAN

Drives no stage-coach He never broke a bank. He has never been known to dress up as a jockey, or try practical jokes on watermen, or empty flour-bags on chimney-sweeps. He shuns cross-barred trowsers, horticultural scarfs, overgrown pins, and can wear a waist coat without a cable's length of gold chain round it. His linen is not illustrated, but beautifully clean. He never does "a little discounting," nor lend his hand to "flying a kite." His aversion for a Gent is softened by pity. He can look at a lady without the aid of an eye-glass. He allows a performer to talk louder than himself at the Theatre, and does not spring on the stage if there is a row at the Opera. He abhors a lie as he does a sheriff's officer. He is not prodigal of oaths, and is equally sparing of perfume. He does not borrow his

English from the stables, and never puts his lips through a dreary fashionable course of lisping. He is not too proud to walk, or to carry an umbrella if it rains, and never waltzes with spurs after supper, even in uniform. He never bets beyond his means, and is not fond of playing high at cards. He never ruined a young man—to say nothing worse. He bows scrupulously, even to a crossing-sweeper. He never shrinks from an I. O. U., nor is afraid of a bill, nor seized with a sudden shortness of memory at the sight of an old friend, whose coat is not so young as it used to be. He has never proved his cowardice by fighting a duel, giving satisfaction always in a more gentlemanly way. He pays for his clothes, disdaining to wear his tailor's in consideration for valuable introductions. His horses, too, are his own, and not purchased of his friends by a series of profitable exchanges. He is not madly attached to billiard-rooms, nor is he seen at Casinos. He locks up his conquests in his own heart, and his love-letters in his desk, rarely disclosing either to his most intimate friends. He does not bully his servants, nor joke with them, nor cut a man because his father was in trade. He is not obsequious to a lord, nor does he hang on the skirts of the aristocracy, knowing that a man's nobility does not depend entirely upon his title, however old and unstained it may be. He travels to enjoy himself, and does not attempt to crush poor foreigners with English gold or pride. He values a thing, not by its price, but by its real value, and does not blush to drink beer if he is thirsty. He does not think it essential to his reputation to keep late hours, to pull down sign boards, bait policemen, and besiege toll-keepers, during the night. He has no such violent love for door-knockers as to induce him to collect them He is not facetious with waiters, or given to knock down a cab-man by way of settling a fare. He is not afraid of laughing if he is amused, even in public, or of handing down an old lady with a turban to dinner, or dancing with his wife. He likes quiet, but does not hate children, and thinks a seat in the House of Com mons not worth the bribery and continual riot. He was never the hero of any wager, riding, running, racing, rowing, eating, or swimming, and does not know a single prize-fighter. He is fond of amuse ments, but does not instal himself at the Opera every night, because it is fashionable. He follows the races; but goes down without a dog-cart and a key-bugle. He is unobtrusive in his dress, and very retired in his jewellery, and has an antipathy for a white hat with a black band, and all violent contradictions either in dress or conversation. He is generous, but does not give grand dinners and expensive suppers to persons he does not know or care about. He lends money; and, if he borrows any, he makes a strange practice of returning it. He rarely "speaks his mind," and is very timid in rushing into a quarrel, of husband and wife especially. He is a favourite with the ladies, but does not put too much starch in his politeness, or too much sugar in his compliments. In matters of scandal he is dumb, if not exactly deaf, and in the rumours, he only believes half (the kinder half, too) of what he hears. He is not prejudiced himself, but has a kind toleration for the prejudices of others. His golden rule is never to hurt the feelings of anybody, or to injure a living creature. All his actions, all his sentiments, are shaped to that noble end; and he dies, as he lives, *sans peur et sans reproche.* His great creed is to do unto others as he would wish others to do unto him. This is the MODEL GENTLEMAN

*Ni con pluma . Ni con pinzel.*

*C'est vainement que l'on presume,*
*Dégaler ce divin sujet;*
*Puis qu'il n'est ny pinceau ny plume,*
*Qui puisse en exprimer un trait.*

[This engraving is copied from a rare old work, published at Paris in 1647, called "*La Galerie des Femmes Fortes*, par le Pierre le Moyne, de la Compagnie de Jesus."]

## A MODEL IRISH SPEAKER

OW have we been treated for the last ten thousand years by the cold blooded Saxon? My hair stands on end to tell you. (*Cheers.*) Hasn't England so managed matters in her own favour that she receives the light of the sun two-and-twenty minutes before she permits a single ray to come to us? (*A Voice; "It's true!"*) England may boast of her own enlightenment; but is this justice to Ireland? (*Tremendous Cries of "No! No!"*) I have next to accuse England of keeping aloof from us fully sixty miles at the nearest point. Talk of our Union after that! (*Vociferous cheering, which lasted several hours.*) No, my countrymen, it is only a parchment Union, a lying thing, made of the skin of the innocent sheep; but, before we go to bed this night we'll see that bit of parchment torn into countless strips, so that every tailor in Ireland shall have, to-morrow morning, a remnant of it in his hands, to measure twelve millions of happy Irishmen with. (*At this point the proceedings were interrupted by six persons being carried out of the room who had fainted. They are supposed to be tailors.*) Well, sir, I denounce from this place the atrocious cupidity of England, by which she monopolises the tin mines entirely, almost all the iron and coal, and thus cramps, sir, our native industry and commerce. Why has not Ireland her own iron and coal? (*Cries of "Why not?"*) I ask, again, why have we no tin? (*"Shame! shame!"*) and no brass? no zinc? no salmon? no elephants? no periwinkles? no king? (*Immense cheering, during which the honourable speaker sat down and slept for a quarter of an hour, and then continued.*) Oh! my beloved countrymen, I have had a most beautiful vision. I thought I saw every field of Ireland covered with dancing corn, and embroidered with the most beautiful sheep, whose wool was more exquisite than all the Berlin wool that was ever made in England (*Cheers*); and I thought, my countrymen, its rivers were filled with more salmon and more periwinkles than ever carolled on the muddy Saxon shore (*Cheers*); and I thought, my countrymen, that on the brow of every other hill the mighty elephant was reposing under the peaceful shade of the shamrock (*more cheers*); and again, I thought the corner of each field was filled with more iron, and tin, and brass than would suffice to build a railway from here to the bottom of England's perdition (*Laughter and Cheers*); and I thought—may the beautiful vision he never effaced from the iris of my weeping eyes!—that there were no dark clouds such as now lour o'er our bright country, but that the whole scene, so intensely Irish, was illumined, as if with a resplendent sun, with our own gas. (*Enthusiastic shouts, the echoes of which have not yet subsided in the neighbourhood of the Castle.*) Oh! oh! when will this vision be realised? When shall we see the poor Irishman—the finest peasant of the world—boiling his potato? Ah! the plundering Saxon cannot wring *that* from us; though no thanks to the monster for the blight—(*Shame*)—boiling his potato, I say, with his own coal, in a pot made of his own iron, and eat it on a plate made of his own pewter, with a knife bought with his own tin. Never! never! until the Repeal is carried. (*Three cheers for Repale.*) Do you think you'll ever have it? ("*We will; we will.*") Believe me, in all sincerity, you never will, until you pull up the lamp-posts and make bayonets of them, and have wrenched off every knocker and bell pull, and melted them into bullets and cannon-balls. (*Cheers.*) I know I am talking sedition; but I dare them to come and tear the shoestrings out of my boots, before I unsay a single word of what I have said. (*Frantic applause.*) They dare not prosecute me It would be the proudest moment for Ireland, if they would; for then College Green would be crowded with Irish kings. (*Cheers.*) The British oak would be supplanted with the four-leaved shamrock of Ireland. (*Cheers.*) The Queen of England would be an Irishwoman—(*Cheers*)—and I should die happy in the thought that the majestic tree of Repeal had been watered with my blood, and blossomed, and borne such golden fruit, that unborn nations, far from beyond the poles, were coming on their knees to taste them. (*It is impossible to describe the enthusiasm which broke out when the Hon. Gentleman resumed his seat on the ledge of the window. As many as had hats, threw them into the air; those who had coats, took them off, and dragged them along the ground; whilst a few of the hardiest natives were observed to bury their faces in their coat-tails, and weep audibly. The cheering was kept up till a very late hour, and the meeting broke up a little before daylight, after giving ninety-nine cheers, and a little one in, "for the blessed cause of Repale."*)

## THE MODEL BANKER.

**HE** IS educated at Eton, and makes love to lords. They borrow his money, and laugh at him, as "a toady." He enters the banking-house at twenty-one, and looks upon the clerks as servants — as breathing copying machines. He belongs to all sorts of clubs. He is a great authority upon wines, horses, and women. He keeps his yacht, and never stops in town after the Opera. He walks through the City as if it belonged to him. He is great in jewellery, and very particular about his riding-whips. He wears in winter white cords and buckskin gloves, and subscribes to the nearest "hounds." His wristbands show an inch and a half. He marries a baronet's daughter, and talks nothing but the Blue Book ever afterwards

He has a house in Belgravia, and a seat in the North He has noisy luncheons in the "parlour." His dinners elicit a little paragraph of praise from the *Morning Post*. His name, too, is generally amongst the "fashionables whom we observed last night at Her Majesty's Theatre." He has always a particular engagement at the West-end at two, at which hour his bay cob invariably calls for him. His printed charities are very extensive — one sum always for himself, another for the Co. He is very nervous during panics, and when there is a run upon the bank, it is always owing to "the pressure of the times." He pays his creditors half-a-crown in the pound, and lives on the £3,000 a-year "settled on his wife." We never knew a Model Banker fall yet, that his fall was not agreeably softened by a snug little property "settled upon his wife." From this we infer that the Model Banker is a most rigid cultivator of the matrimonial virtues, and if he forgets occasionally what he owes to himself and to others, he remembers to a nicety what is due to his wife. It is only the system of Double Entry applied to Banking.

# THE MODEL SPONGE.

As the dinner-hour strikes, the Sponge knocks at the door Sometimes he brings a bag of filberts with him. The host thanks him, and produces sundry bottles of his best port. Sometimes he sends a hare. He knows that the first rule of society is, that whoever sends a hare is necessarily invited to dinner. Sometimes it a box for the play. The result is always the same. The sponge knows all the secret springs of the heart and the stomach (they too frequently lodge together), which, ever so slightly touched upon, draw out a

gratuitous dinner. His conversation, too, is got up
as neatly as himself. His fronts are richer than those
of Regent Street. His jokes, also, are beautifully
dressed. His scandal (for the ladies) is always of the
newest cut, and his anecdotes fit as if they had been
measured expressly for the company. He leaves early
He has a tea in the neighbourhood—a dear friend
who is ill. He does not stop long, however, for he
recollects he knows a hot supper just close by. He
carves — his manœuvres with the knife and fork
exercise, in fact, are perfect — helps everybody to a
nicety, and does not forget the old proverb which
says, that he who wishes to be helped in this
world must, first of all, help himself oo he keeps
the liver wing for himself. He goes home with
a stranger, and breakfasts with him. He remembers, however, about two o'clock, that he has business
in the City. His visit occurs, curiously enough, just
at luncheon time. He is invited "to pick a bone,"
and devours a chicken. "The air of the City is so
bracing." His appetite is most accommodating. Its
range seems to exceed even that of Soyer's kitchen at
the Reform Club. He likes everything. Cold meat
does not daunt him A large family does not terrify
him. Saturday, however, is the day of the week he
likes the least. It is the day of hashes, of make-shifts,
of pickles, bread-pudding, and liver and bacon. Sunday
is his grand day, but he gives the preference of his
society to those houses which do not involve a walk,
or a cab, or an omnibus home. At his own house he
is—but here we must drop the Sponge, for we would

not go home with him for any price. We cannot fancy a Sponge sponging upon himself; the sight would be awful. To be properly appreciated, the Sponge must be seen at other persons' tables. He fattens the best in town. The country offers too large a field for his exploits, which, unless he keeps a horse, he cannot possibly get over, or bag more than one meal a day. He is the gentleman-greengrocer who attends dinners, and waits at evening-parties without the fee.

# THE MODEL LODGER.

HE is a quiet gentleman. A smile is permanently settled on his clean face. He wipes his boots on the mat before he walks up-stairs. He pays a high rent, and has few friends. He leaves his drawers open. He has a cellar of coals in at a time. He takes in a newspaper, and is not in a hurry for it in the morning. He is never out later than ten. He shaves with cold water. He never adds up a bill. He is fond of children. He likes to buy them sweetmeats, and to take one occasionally to the theatre. He never has supper. He never dines at home, excepting on a Sunday, and that rarely. The landlady orders then his dinner: it is generally a very large joint, with plenty of vegetables, a very large pie, and a very large slice of cheese. He never inquires for the joint, or the pie, or anything, the next day. He lends his books cheerfully. He is in doubt about the exact number of his shirts. He rarely rings the bell. He pays for extras without a murmur. Rather likes music. Does not object to a flute and a piano playing different tunes at the same time. He is not particular about his letters being opened. He can eat a cold dinner without salt, pepper, or mustard. He believes in " the cat." He knows nothing will " keep" in warm weather. He keeps a tea-caddy, but has lost the key. He never has his bed warmed. He is never in arrear with his rent: if it is not paid the very day it becomes due, the reason is because he has paid it the day before. The Model Lodger is single, but without friends, with very few knocks at the door; no Irish acquaintances; does not know one medical student He is sheepish, rich, and contented.

# THE MODEL BEADLE

THE Model Beadle's strut is slow and majestic, like a peacock's. You rarely see him running, excepting when there is a very flagrant case of "owdacious wagabonds." He is large, as if he lived on the fat of the Parish. He is good-tempered, excepting during divine service, and then the smallest breach of etiquette makes him suddenly break out with a sort of Beadle-rash all over. His anger, however, is like his cane: if it soon waxes warm, it soon cools again. He wipes his steaming forehead, crosses his legs, and is at peace once more with all the world.

The Model Beadle always looks contemplative. He seems as if his thoughts were feasting upon his dinner, or his muffins, or the bit of tripe that is waiting for him at home. His face is a rich larder of content.

His lips are apparently imbued with a perpetual motion of eating and drinking. His eyes shine as with the lustre of soup. His cheeks are swollen like beefsteak puddings, as if they were the unctuous tombs of many rich things. His nose is a small station, buried between two high embankments of fat. How happy he looks! He seems as if he had been born great, instead of having greatness only thrust upon him. You imagine he came into the world a Beadle, like Minerva, ready armed, with cocked hat and highlows, and that he cut his teeth with a Beadle's staff.

Yet he is tender as he is great, like a prize ox. He conducts a donkey to the pound with the same gentleness that he holds a baby at the font. He will give away a bride, or stand godfather, merely for the asking He is not proud, though he may look it. He will hold a silver plate at a charity sermon, and put on a pair of Berlin gloves for the occasion. He will take a shilling, too, just as readily as the pew-opener. He is fond of sleep, but can keep his eyes open during an entire sermon—if it is the Bishop's. He is rarely upset. excepting by a bit of orange-peel, when his greatness feels the fall most heavily. But the flies annoy him the most in summer. On a hot day they sting him almost to madness. He rolls about on his seat as uneasy as a Frenchman on a steam-packet. He raises his mighty hand against them—the blow falls on his massive forehead, and resounds again, like hail against a window. His face vies in burning crimson with his cape; but does a single murmur escape his lips? No!—he forgives, and builds himself up against a pillar for another snooze; till a big bluebottle drives him into the churchyard for fresh air; and there the invigorating sight of boys playing at leapfrog on a Sunday soon wakes him up, and the Beadle feels himself again.

little ned

Old Geffris

ante e A rummun on

HISTORICAL CARTOON, DISCOVERED ON THE WALLS OF A METROPOLITAN CHURCH.

The Model Beadle does not make himself too cheap. He knows his sphere, and like a gold fish (that pictorial model of himself—vermilion turned up with gold) in a bowl, he has the sense to keep within it. He has the tenacity of ivy for the church. If he is not standing under the portico, basking in the sun, his legs astride like a full-dress Colossus, he is cooling himself in one of the free seats;—if not in the vestry, tasting the wine, he is meditating amongst the tombs

His reading takes in an extensive range of epitaphs.
He wanders through a maze of granite virtues, and
thinks in his heart the world is peopled, like a
churchyard, with nothing but affectionate wives,
deeply-lamented husbands, and inconsolable widows;
but is rather puzzled to think how folks can be so
happy, since every one dies "universally regretted."

The Beadle's amusements are limited. His notions
of the funny are evidently buried in the grave. He
is too dignified to laugh. As for dancing—you might
as well expect St. Paul's to do the egg-hornpipe. He
lives by himself, within himself, for himself. He
passes Punch and Judy without a pause, without a
smile. Jack-in-the-Green makes him move down
another street. Guy Faux is to him only a blaze of
nonsense, though he looks more warmly upon that
than anything else—for he has a suspicion that it is
an institution in some way connected with the church
The Beadle in the drama of Punch is his horror; and
he would certainly take him into custody, with the
show, drum, pandean-pipes, and all, if he only dared
The Beadle may be the source of fun to others, but he
has no appreciation of fun himself. Who ever saw a
Beadle at a theatre? But he smiles, sometimes,
when there is a christening of twins.

He is not gregarious either. He is rarely
seen with other Beadles. The sight of two Beadles
would create astonishment—three together would
cause a crowd. He mostly walks by himself, as if
no one ought to divide the pavement with him.
Watch him at the head of a charity procession—or at

a charity dinner—or when he is beating the bounds—
or on a board day—or on any grand or festive occasion
—you will see he generally keeps himself to himself
Omnibusses, steamboats, or tea-gardens, rarely see him
inside. It is the curse of Greatness to have no friends.
The only occasion he mixes with human beings is
on a " Dreadful Conflagration." He puts himself then,
without pride, at the head of the parish engine. He
encourages the boys—he whips himself into a small
canter—he stands out all the larger before a fire.
He lights up with the flames. His consequence
seems to expand, and his cocked hat to grow bigger,
as the little regiment of ragamuffins (with whom, on
any other occasion, he would not march through
Coventry Court) joyfully cry, " Hoorah !" Napoleon
crossing the Bridge of Lodi was not more sublime
than he is running up the door-steps to call upon the
inhabitants within to surrender, or else they will be
burnt to the ground.—By-the-bye, has it ever been
remarked that the costume of the Beadle is not at all
unlike that of the Emperor? The same cocked-hat
exactly—the same coat and cape precisely. The
parallel between the two might be carried further; but
we are sure the Beadle would not like it.

The Model Beadle loves a nosegay. He has a
proud affection for his gold-lace, and keeps it as
bright as his staff. Every one of his large buttons,
too, is a mirror to shave in. His calves, somehow,
always keep clean. Another of his peculiarities is the
wiry straightness of his hair. Another oddity lurks in
his eye—for it divides with Irish guns the faculty of

shooting round the corner. It can scowl at a charity boy two streets off. There is a doll-like cleanliness about him. His face shines like wax—no bit of straw, no stain, no speck of dirt, ever disfigures his purple face or fine linen. The dust, even, seems to respect him. He is so neat, you fancy he has just been taken out of a bandbox—though it must have been rather a large one to have contained him.

He hates boys—charity-boys especially; but does not allow his anger to carry him away too far. He generally stops when he has lost his breath. This is the reason probably that the boys who are caught suffer for those who are not caught. It is false that he eats the oranges and apples he takes from them—he gives them to his children; for the Beadle has a wife at home, who smoothes his ruffled brow, and irons his rumpled handkerchief, after the scuffles and the heats of the feverish day. He buries under his pillow all the stones and slights which his order has long received as a patrimony from the hands of Society; and on his virtuous bed is wafted to the happy land of dreams—But stop, does the Beadle ever go to bed? It is so hard to imagine a Beadle without his clothes. He must sleep in his cocked hat.

Model Reader, do not despise the Beadle. For centuries he has been subjected to persecutions. Every Boy's hand is raised against him—every Man's nose is turned up at him. It is time the Beadle's Disabilities were repealed, and the Pariah of the Parish was pressed to every one's bosom as a Man and a Brother.

ße kind to him—listen to his poetry at Christmas, and give him half-a-crown. Do not invariably snub him when he serves you with a summons;—offer him a trifle at Easter, when he collects the offerings;—go up and exchange a few words with him when you meet him;—ask him occasionally what he will have to drink—and it is astonish-
ing the deal of gentleness you will find hidden in the austere nature of this paro-chial Dr. Johnson. All that glitters about the Beadle is not pride. Tear off the heavy coating of gold, and you will find the solid gin-gerbread of the man under-neath. Make an effort, and you cannot fail to love the MODEL BEADLE.

AN old cynic will say, "Pooh! the race is extremely rare—just as rare as a race between two 'busses is frequent." Yet, there is such a being! He gets to the Bank quicker than you can walk it. He wears worsted gloves, but no holes in the tips. He is acquainted with the difference between Kennington and Kensington. He does not put old ladies into the 'bus first, and inquire where they are going to afterwards. He can stop at a

"public" on the roadside without having a pipe and
a game of billiards. He keeps a good supply of
coppers, and when he does give change for a sovereign
there is not a bad sixpence in it. He respects the
slender frames of bandboxes, and does not turn bird-
cages upside down. He hands in a dog or a baby
without pinching either. He does not mind taking a
gentleman's umbrella outside, and holding it over
himself if it is very wet. He does not smoke in
broad daylight, nor drink before dinner. He lets an
old gentleman get off the steps before he says "All
right." He allows no butcher-boys to jump up be
hind He uses the manual telegraph but slightly
He never dances on his footboard, excepting it is the
double shuffle in cold weather, to keep his foot warm
The only thing that tempts him off his bracket is a
good slide in winter. He does not know every house-
maid that is making beds or cleaning windows along
the road; can pass a hearse without telling the driver
to "look alive;" nor is he particular in inquiring of
every cabman with a white hat, whether he was the
identical individual " vot stole the donkey?" He
allows a lady an unlimited number of bundles and
babies; and, if it is raining cats and dogs (or mutton
pies, as he calls it), he does not object—if the passen-
gers do not—to a washerwoman taking her basket inside. He can only count up to eighteen; all beyond
that number he puts down, or else carries over to the
next 'bus. He is only Minister of the Interior. The
Exterior, viz., the box seat, is to him quite a Foreign
Department, of which the driver only has the reins

But the roof of an omnibus is, like the deck of a steamer, built to hold any number, so he always has room for one outside. He is exceedingly gallant, and is always asking " if any gentleman minds going on the roof, just to oblige a lady." His badge is so bright it shines like a medal of good conduct. He wears it proudly on his breast, like a lady's locket. He is free from that other badge of his order—imposition. If the price is threepence, he does not take you a kerb-stone further to space it into sixpence. He does not extort a shilling under the mean pretext that it is Sunday. He is sparing in his dialogue with " Bill" (all drivers' names are Bill) touching what he did last night at the " Heagle." He is too gentlemanly to pull a lady's boa to pieces, or to struggle for half a shawl; but if he is contending with a refractory rival for the possession of a fare, his great *coup de main* always is to run off with the baby and put it inside his 'bus, and gallop on. The result invariably proves his elegant prediction—" that it must be a precious bad cow that will not follow its calf," for the next moment there is an agonizing cry of " Stop," and sure enough it is the panting mother shouting to the conductor, like the witches in Macbeth, " Hail! all hail!" This only proves his love for children. You seldom see him peeling a hot potato on his pedestal, though it is a luxury he is very fond of, as proved by his never reaching the end of a journey without tossing for one. He is above fear, and only laughs when a 'bus behind tries to stir him up with its long pole. He does not climb on to the roof when a big black bull sniffs the straw on which he is standing. He is above cruelty, and jumps as quick as a lightning conductor to help an old woman whose apple-stall has been knocked over by "too close a shave" of the wheel. He knows his station, and holds discourse with no smart cook that is sitting next the door, and was never known to lie down on the plush cushions, excepting it was the last 'bus home, and it was pitch dark, and there was not a "Hangel," or a "Goat in Boots" left inside

Such is the Model Omnibus Conductor—without paint, without varnish, without "chaff," that ill-grained commodity which his fellow-badgers generally "sow broadcast" through the streets of London. He knows perfectly well that where there is chaff there must be thrashing, and, as he is not anxious to bring this about his ears, he leaves those green fields to be taken up with the "rigs" of others. Such is his lofty career—he shuts his door against no man—his hand is held out to the richest and the poorest. If you have dropped a sixpence in the straw, he will bring a light and look for it. If you are wise, you will take his number, for you may spend a whole fortune in omnibusses before you will meet with another MODEL OM-NIBUS CONDUCTOR!

## A SMALL GROUP OF MODELS.

THE MODEL PET PARSON has the most beautiful black hair, and the prettiest loves of whiskers. He attends tea and whist parties, and preaches in canary-coloured kid gloves, with the most dazzling diamond outside his little finger. He has the smallest fashionable lisp in the world. He is highly eau-de-Cologned. His handkerchief is of the purest cambric—a perfect cobweb, edged with lace. He is never without a "nervous headache." He is very delicate, poor fellow! He lives on cold chicken and white wine whey. He rides to church in a lady's carriage. He is supported by the voluntary contributions of the young ladies of the neighbourhood, and has embroidered braces sufficient to stock the whole of the Highlands. Hassocks, too, book-marks and covers, orange marmalade, calf's-foot jelly, grapes, game, tea-cakes, and sweet-breads, of all varieties, are left "for his kind acceptance" every day. He collects pennies for converted washerwomen. He and the Duke of Wellington have married more "lovely brides" than the whole Church. His dress is profound black, relieved with liberal wristbands, and a shirt-front that sticks out like the paper ornament of a fire-grate. When he gets preferment to a more fashionable church, a magnificent silver teapot is presented to him by the ladies, with a beautiful purse full of new sovereigns. With the purity of his white neckcloth, the Pet Parson is sure of a rich wife, and innumerable legacies.

THE MODEL ACTOR speaks the words of Shakspere in preference to his own. He is free from the theatrical superstition that genius is found at the bottom of a brandy bottle. He estimates talent by a higher measurement than the letters in the play-bills. He is not inflated with the belief that he ought to act *Macbeth* every night. In going through his lines he is not continually falling over a " Ha-ha !" nor does he embroider all his sentences with a running " Hem!" He does not appeal to the " skey," or his " kynd" friends. He refuses to appear in low neck, bare arms, and woman's clothes, thinking that an actor always studies his character best when he is acting the part of a gentleman.

THE MODEL BARRISTER returns his fees, let them be ever so large, when he has not been able to attend to his Brief.

THE MODEL PREMIER.—No such person ever known.

THE MODEL BORE.—You're another.

THE MODEL DONKEY.—He is to be heard of in the House of Commons.

THE MODEL COUSIN.—The Servant's Best Friend.

THE MODEL BEGGAR.—For list of candidates, see the Pension List.

The Model Quack does not take his own medicine—only writes the testimonials.

The Model Humbug —The claims are too numerous to decide

The Model Cabman keeps his temper if offered an eightpenny fare.

The Model Doctor can go to church without being called out in the middle of the service.

The Model Manager.—You had better inquire of the Drury Lane Committee; or a shorter cut probably will be to go at once to the Insolvent Debtors' Court. Search till you succeed.

The Model Author.—Ask the first author you meet, and there cannot be a doubt about it

The Model Publisher.—*Vide* our title-page.

# Advertising Sheet.

## CHRISTMAS PRESENTS.

The exuberance of the feelings amidst scenes of gaiety induces the fair and youthful to shine to advantage under the gaze of many friends, and therefore to devote increased attention to the duties of the Toilet. It is at this festive season that

## ROWLANDS' AUXILIARIES OF HEALTH & BEAUTY

are more than usually essential.

The patronage of Royalty throughout Europe, their general use by Rank and Fashion, and the universally-known efficacy of these articles give them a celebrity unparalleled, and render them peculiarly

## ELEGANT & SEASONABLE PRESENTS.

## ROWLANDS' MACASSAR OIL

Is a delightfully fragrant and transparent preparation for the hair, and as an invigorator and beautifier beyond all precedent.

In dressing the Hair nothing can equal its effect, rendering it so admirably soft, that it will lie in any direction, and imparting a transcendant lustre.—Price 3s. 6d., 7s.; Family Bottles (equal to four small) 10s. 6d., and double that size, 21s. per bottle.

## ROWLANDS' KALYDOR,
### FOR THE SKIN AND COMPLEXION,

Is unequalled for its rare and inestimable qualities, the radiant bloom it imparts to the cheek, the softness and delicacy which it induces of the hands and arms, its capability of soothing irritation, and removing cutaneous defects, discolorations, and all unsightly appearances, render it

### INDISPENSABLE TO EVERY TOILET.
Price 4s. 6d. and 8s. 6d. per bottle.

## ROWLANDS' ODONTO,
### OR PEARL DENTIFRICE,
### FOR PRESERVING AND BEAUTIFYING THE TEETH

*Imparting to them a Pearl-like Whiteness, Strengthening the Gums, and for rendering the Breath sweet and pure.*

Price 2s. 9d. per box.

---

### \*\*\* Sold by A. ROWLAND and SONS,
20, HATTON GARDEN, LONDON,
AND BY CHEMISTS AND PERFUMERS.

### \*\*\* Beware of Spurious Imitations!!